For Ciara, Nathan, Dominic—B.F.M.
For Varja and Marusja—A.R.

Copyright © 1998 by Nord-Süd Verlag AG, Gossau Zürich, Switzerland
First published in Switzerland under the title *Bärenweihnacht*.
English translation copyright © 1998 by North-South Books Inc.

All rights reserved. No part of this book may be reproduced or utilized
in any form or by any means, electronic or mechanical, including
photocopying, recording, or any information storage and retrieval
system, without permission in writing from the publisher.

First published in the United States, Great Britain, Canada,
Australia, and New Zealand in 1998 by North-South Books,
an imprint of Nord-Süd Verlag AG, Gossau Zürich, Switzerland.

Library of Congress Cataloging-in-Publication Data is available.
A CIP catalogue record for this book is available from The British Library.
ISBN 1-55858-971-6 (trade binding) 10 9 8 7 6 5 4 3 2 1
ISBN 1-55858-972-4 (library binding) 10 9 8 7 6 5 4 3 2 1
Printed in Belgium

For more information about our books, and the authors and artists
who create them, visit our web site: http://www.northsouth.com

Brigitte Frey Moret

The Bear's Christmas

Illustrated by Alexander Reichstein

Translated by Rosemary Lanning

North-South Books
New York · London

Once upon a time, long, long ago, bears did
not hide away and sleep through the winter. Instead,
they roamed the forests, hunting for food.

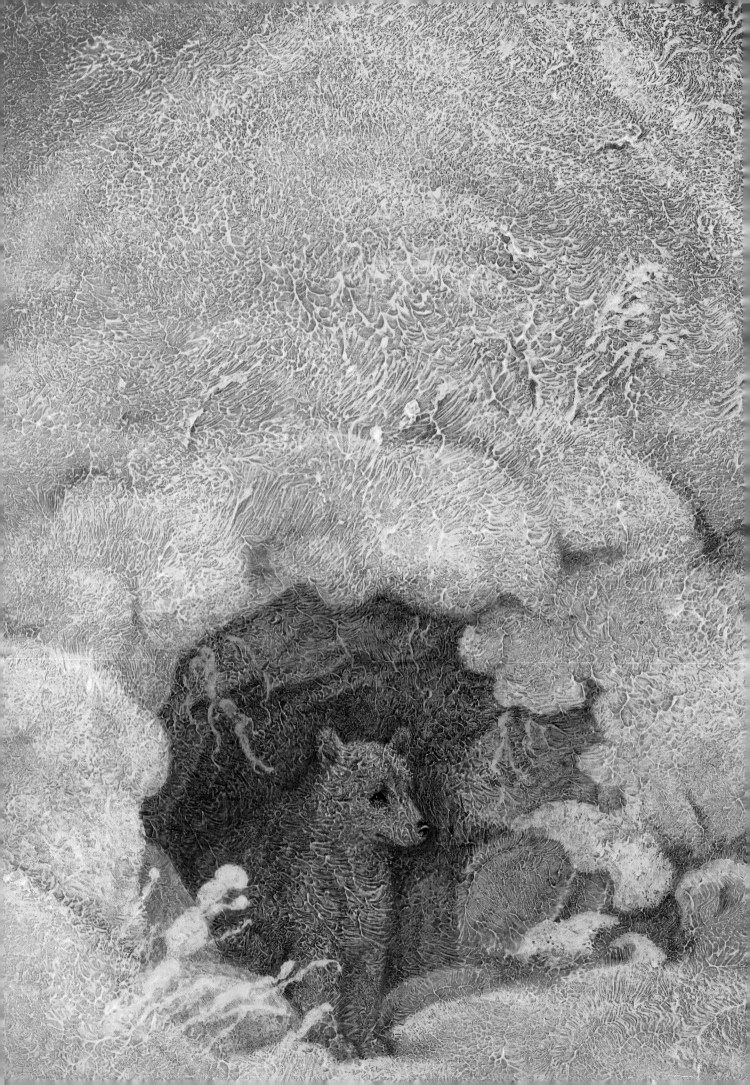

In those long-ago times, a young bear lived
in a cave in the mountains. On winter days he often
found no food at all. Then he was so hungry
that he could not sleep.

One night the bear climbed a high rock and stared
out over the ice and snow. He saw no sign of life anywhere.
Nothing moved in the cold darkness. The other animals
were all asleep in their shelters.

The bear saw a faint glow in the
distance—a shepherd's campfire perhaps.
Hunger drew him towards the light. The bear
crouched low as he came to the edge of the forest.
Beyond the trees lay a pasture. He could smell sheep.

One lamb had moved away from the flock. The bear watched it closely. The lamb seemed unaware of danger as it calmly rooted for green plants under the snow. The bear tensed, ready to spring . . .

when suddenly a bright light filled the sky.
From all around came the sound of glorious singing.
The bear stood still and listened, spellbound, to the
angels' song. He forgot his hunger, forgot the lamb.

The song came to an end, and the angels vanished.
The shepherds swiftly gathered their flocks, took
their kettle from the fire, and set off over the hills.
The bear followed them, as if in a dream, across
the snowy fields and frozen streams.

The night sky had grown bright. The bear
saw a brilliant star shining over a stable and
once again he heard the glorious singing.

The air seemed full of
sweetness, like honey.

The bear gazed at the stable from afar. It was
bathed in a warm glowing light. He saw a woman
inside with a baby wrapped in her cloak.

The woman looked up and saw the bear. She seemed to know at once what he needed, and she beckoned to him. The bear hesitated, then walked toward her. The sheep and the shepherds fearfully drew aside and let him pass.

But the woman was not afraid. She held out
a small branch, bearing a few red berries. The bear
began to eat, trembling with joy at the berries'
sweetness. Instantly his hunger was satisfied.
He gave a low growl of gratitude …

and went back to his cave.
There he curled up and drifted into a deep sleep.
He did not wake until the warmth of spring
crept into his cave once again.

Ever since that night bears have loved sweet red berries.
And ever since that night they have slept all winter long.